The Magic Soap Bubble

David Cory

Edition : Culturea (Hérault, 34)
Contact : infos@culturea.fr
Print in Germany by Books on Demand
Design and layout : Derek Murphy
Layout : Reedsy (https://reedsy.com/)
ISBN : 9791041828036
Légal deposit : July 2023

The Magic Soap Bubble

THE MAGIC SOAP PIPE

NED had been reading a very interesting book about fairies and goblins, and how these real queer little folk inhabit dense forests and lofty mountain caves and lead a wonderful life apart from the homes and cities of men.

The book was very large and heavy, and the afternoon was very warm, and the big armchair in which he was curled up was so comfortable that by and by he let the book slip to one side.

He had just closed his eyes for a moment to rest them, when he was startled by a little squeaky voice at his elbow.

He opened his eyes with a start and saw a Gnome standing on the window-sill just in front of him. Yes, there was no mistake about it, it was a Gnome. For had not Ned a moment before seen his picture in the big book he had been reading? Indeed, it almost seemed as if the picture itself had stepped out of the page from between the covers, so exactly a duplicate did the little man appear.

"Hello, Ned!" said the little squeaky voice again. "I say, hello! You ought to know me well enough by this time to answer, since you've been reading about me for the last hour."

"Hello, yourself!" replied Ned, laughing in spite of himself, and rubbing his eyes again to make sure that it was not a picture from the book.

"Can't you see a fellow is sleepy after reading so long a time? I didn't think you were coming out of the book to speak to me, you know."

"Neither did I," retorted the Gnome, with a funny wink. "I came from the forest to invite you to take a little journey with me through Gnomeland. I am the King of the Gnomes, and my subjects have told me how interested you are in reading about us, so I have come to take you for a trip through our kingdom. I know you will love to see all the wonderful things you have been reading about. Will you come?"

"Indeed, I will," said Ned.

"Then follow me," replied the Gnome.

Ned jumped through the window after the little fellow, who ran swiftly down the walk and across the fields to the forest beyond.

As they neared the brook that ran through the meadow, the Gnome paused. Taking from his pocket a clay pipe, he stooped over and filled it with water.

"Did you ever blow soap bubbles?" he asked, taking a piece of soap from another pocket and rubbing it carefully around the inside of the pipe-bowl.

"Yes," replied Ned, "lots of times."

"Well, you wait and see what sort of a bubble I'll blow," replied the Gnome.

It was a bubble! But the strangest part of it all was that Ned found himself inside of it with his companion.

"How did we get inside, or how did the bubble get around us?" asked Ned, but before his question was answered away went the bubble up in the air, across the meadow, above the little brook, yes, over the roof of his own house, higher and higher, until finally it reached the big high mountain that he had so often dimly seen from the window of his bedroom at home.

After circling about the highest peak the bubble at length safely landed on a rocky ledge.

Before Ned could ask how they were ever going to get out the Gnome opened a little door through which he led him to the outer air.

There was a great change in the temperature, or else the inside of the bubble was very warm, for Ned began to shiver and shake. "Who-o-!" he cried; "it's co-old!"

"Of course it is. Look," answered the Gnome, and Ned's eyes, following the pointing finger of his little friend, fell upon a strange and terrifying figure.

Behind a bank of icicles stood a giant, with an immense helmet upon his head, from which hung long sharp pieces of ice. The top part was covered with snow which slipped off at intervals like a small avalanche to the ground below. His beard and mustache were festooned with thin slivers of ice, and his shoulders bore epaulets of frosted snow. The cuffs of his greatcoat were fringed with snowflakes, and altogether he was a startling and frigid looking individual. In his hands he held a monstrous bellows, from which he forced out a blast of icy air which, scattering the snow in whirling clouds, went howling down the rocky ravines.

"He's the Wind Man of the Mountain," explained the Gnome, turning to shivering Ned, whose toes and fingers by this time were quite numb with the cold.

"Well, I'd like to meet a Hot Air Man," said Ned, blowing on his hands to keep them from freezing. "I'd like to feel warm again."

"Well, then follow me!" cried the Gnome, and turning to a big rock he tapped upon it twice with the toe of his little red boot. In a moment a dooropened, showing a pair of rocky steps leading down into the mountain.

"Be careful," admonished the Gnome, as he and Ned descended the rough flight. "Don't slip, for you might fall a long way."

Ned assured him he had no desire to fall, but that his feet were so numb he wasn't at all sure but what he might slip, no matter how hard he tried to be careful.

Although it was not exactly dark, at the same time the light was not sufficient for Ned to make out anything distinctly, and as the stairway was narrow and the walls dim he kept his eyes closely upon the ground.

Soon they came to a level corridor and he perceived a dim light in the distance. "Where are we going?" he asked. But at this point an iron door arrested their progress, and without pausing to answer, the Gnome took from his pocket a key. Inserting it in the lock, the door slowly swung open, and Ned heard the faint beating of a drum.

"Sit down," said the Gnome, drawing forward a wooden stool, much too small for Ned, but probably just the right size for a Gnome; "sit down and wait a moment while I go in search of the Gnomeland Band. I want you to hear them play, and I hear them practising now."

Ned glanced curiously around the strange place. It suddenly occurred to him that he was a long, long way from home. Here he was, deep down in the mountain, in a rocky cavern, sitting on a little Gnome stool, waiting for his friend to return. But what if he did not come back?

Ned's hair suddenly stood on end at the thought. Going over to the big iron door, he tried to turn the great knob, but his fingers either were not strong enough or he did not know the secret of the lock. Returning to his seat, he made up his mind to wait a while before allowing his fears to get the better of him. This is what every brave boy would do under the circumstances, he said to himself, resolving not to be a coward.

Presently he was relieved to hear music, as the Gnome, at the head of the Gnomeland Band, came into view; and the funniest band that Ned had ever seen. Why, each instrument was playing itself and dancing the Mountain Tango at the same time!

The big drum went "Bum, bum, bum, diddle dum," and pranced around on a pair of short, fat legs in red stockings. Two fat little arms beat the drumsticks on the top of his head, or what appeared to be the top of his head, which was in reality a funny face, which winked and blinked as the drumsticks traveled over the queer little features.

"Toot! toot!" went the big yellow horn, as his fat little fingers pressed in the brass stops that made the notes high or low, or soft or shrill. Over the floor he skipped, after the round, fat drum.

The 'cello and the violin came next. The latter ran his bow across his stringed waistcoat in perfect time, while the former twanged the strings that covered his happy face in a jolly fashion. The rest of the band played on themselves beautifully, and the Gnome, with his baton, proved a most capable leader. In fact, the music was so delightful that Ned finally could restrain himself no longer, and, jumping up, began dancing around to the tune of "For He's a Jolly Good Fellow!"

"Heigh-ho! hey diddle-do!

Down in the mountain deep,

Fiddle and drum, tiddle-dy-um,

Are doing the Leopard Leap!"

Just then the music stopped, or, rather, the Musical Instruments paused to take breath, and Ned sat down again, wondering what next would happen. In a few minutes the round, fat drum commenced to beat "Left, right! left, right!" and the Gnomeland Band fell into line and marched slowly down the long cavern until it was out of sight.

THE MAGIC CAKE

AS the last drum beat died away in the distance, the Gnome turned to Ned and said: "Come, let us hasten, for I am rather hungry, and you no doubt are in need of nourishment also."

Ned obeyed willingly, for he had tasted nothing since breakfast and was now as hungry as a healthy youngster should be.

At the farther end of the cavern was an inclined plane, very much like the chutes at Coney Island.

Carefully seating Ned at his side the Gnome said: "Now hold tight, and hold your breath and hold your tongue—in fact, hold everything you've got—for we are going to take a swift shoot to the bottom of the mountain and you'll find out what the word swift means if you never have before!"

At this they began to move, and in another moment they were traveling as fast as a bullet from a gun.

The wind, whistling by, cut Ned's cheeks like little sharp needles; his hair stood out behind like feathers on a speeding arrow.

They were going so fast it was almost impossible to breathe.

Presently a tiny light appeared in the distance, and he saw that they were now on a level, although still going at a tremendous rate of speed.

In another moment they shot through the little round hole of light, which turned out to be the opening at the other end, and he and the Gnome landed safely on a big soft bunker of moss in the midst of a beautiful forest.

Birds were singing in the treetops and little rabbits were skipping on the soft carpet of the woodland.

Pretty flowers sent forth a delicious perfume and a brook close at hand rippled over the pebbly bottom of its bed.

"Wait," cried the Gnome, as Ned leaned over to drink the cool water. "Wait; I have for you the most delicious drink if you will restrain your impatience a moment longer."

Ned obeyed and followed the Gnome along a narrow path until they came to a small clearing, where the blue sky smiled down upon them.

In the center of the spot was a monstrous watermelon, standing up on end, the thick vine supporting it like a strong round barrel stave.

A large wooden spigot protruded from one side and over it leaned a Gnome, who had climbed upon the vine in order to reach the handle.

Ned's little companion lifted a goblin cup to catch the drops of delicious looking pink juice which began to drip slowly from the spigot when the Gnome carefully turned the handle.

"Careful, now," commanded the Gnome, as he handed the brimming goblet to Ned. "See that you spill not a drop of the precious nectar.

"Good, is it?" he inquired, seeing the sparkle in Ned's eyes and hearing the smack on his lips as the last drop disappeared. "Pretty good, eh?"

"Better'n soda water," replied Ned; "lots better."

The little Gnome at the spigot smiled. "I grew the melon," he said with pride. "It's the largest so far in Gnomeland. But next year I'm going to grow even a bigger one!"

"How do you make them grow so large?" inquired Ned, hoping he would be invited to have another glass of the juice.

"Not another drop!" said Ned's little friend. "A second goblet and you would be so hungry you could eat stones."

"Come with me," said the small Gnome guide. "We must eat."

Ned eagerly followed him, and they pressed forward at a rapid walk until they came to a queer little hut, from which issued a most delicious odor of sponge cake.

Around the door, or, more properly, what appeared to be one, but which was in fact but a small opening, stood several goblins, evidently awaiting orders from someone.

As Ned drew near he perceived that instead of a hut it was in reality a huge oven, in which something very delicious was being baked.

"Minions!" called out Ned's friend, "is not the goblin cake ready?"

"Yes, sire!" responded several voices, and in another moment the oven was taken apart and removed from the most delicious looking sponge cake that Ned had ever seen. A soft, warm brown color made it most tempting to the eyes, and the delicious smell made Ned so anxious to commence eating that he could with difficulty restrain himself.

"Help yourself," cried his little friend, and without a moment's hesitation Ned pulled off a piece of cake and eagerly commenced.

"Begone!" commanded the Gnome to the small bakers, who still stood around curiously watching their cake disappearing down the mouth of a mortal as rapidly as its owner could cram it in; "begone and leave us to enjoy the cake alone!"

At this they turned away and descended the steep hill which lay to the right and disappeared below.

"Be careful," admonished the Gnome, as Ned showed no signs of finishing, "you may eat too much. Gnome cake, while most delicious, is more filling than that of mortal make!"

But Ned paid no heed. Already he had eaten a great hole in the cake and, finding the inside warm and flaky, he squeezed himself in.

It was much easier to eat the inside, as it was softer, and the crust had already grown quite hard.

He was so busy eating and, I'm sorry to say, so greedy, that he did not notice that as he ate away the interior of the sponge cake the outside gradually grew tighter, and the opening which he had made at the beginning of his feast, and through which he had crowded, became smaller and smaller, until finally it closed altogether.

When Ned perceived this, and it was some time after, I assure you, he was indeed frightened. He pounded on the walls of his sponge cake prison and called loudly to the Gnome, but for some time he heard nothing.

Finally, after frantically running around and around inside the huge cake ball, he thought he heard the voice of his small friend. He pressed his ear close to the wall and listened.

Sure enough, he could just hear the words, "Hold on tight to one side, and brace your feet," and the next moment he perceived that the cake was in motion.

Slowly at first, but in a few minutes the great cake ball began to revolve faster and faster.

Ned was terrified at first, as it was with great difficulty that he kept his body from playing battledore and shuttlecock. The greater the speed of the huge mass, however, the less inclination there was to bounce about, and he soon found himself literally glued, as it were, to one side.

While thus traveling in this novel way, he began to entertain some fear as to what would happen should an obstacle be encountered, and by some strange coincidence no sooner had, the idea come than it was followed by a terrific crash!

The crust of the cake ball broke into a thousand pieces, and Ned landed safely some distance from the spot, still clinging to a huge piece of sponge cake, which acted like a cushion between him and the ground.

Looking anxiously around, after wiping some stray crumbs from his eyes, he saw his little friend, the Gnome, running frantically down the steep incline, which, luckily for Ned, had been the cause of his liberation.

Finding him unhurt, the Gnome sat down on the piece of cake to rest himself and regain his breath before speaking.

When he did, however, what he said caused Ned to run quickly over to the brook to look at himself in the water.

To his dismay, what the Gnome had said was, indeed, too true. Ned was nearly as broad as he was high.

The cake he had eaten had evidently occupied the same space inside of him as it had inside the brown crust.

"What am I ever going to do?" said Ned.

"'Twas a lucky think I kept you from drinking another gobletful of the watermelon juice," answered the Gnome. "Otherwise you might have eaten the whole cake, and then you might have been twice as large as you are now."

"I don't think there is anything to laugh at," said Ned, as his small friend burst into a hearty peal of laughter.

"Of course you don't," replied the Gnome, "you can't see yourself. If you could, though—oh, my!" and he again burst into peals of laughter.

Ned waited a few moments and then asked: "Well, what are we going to do?"

"Don't worry, Ned, dear," replied his little friend, touched by his good nature and feeling sorry for him, "don't worry. The watermelon juice made the sponge cake swell. All that is necessary now is to take the antidote, and I know where it can be found without any trouble."

THE MAGIC NECTAR

NED and the Gnome continued their journey down the valley, following the crystal stream, in whose waters he had just a short time before seen his distorted figure, until they came to a beautiful waterfall, down whose silvery sheen slid numerous water sprites and water fairies.

"Over yonder," exclaimed the Gnome, "lives the Fairy of the Lake. She brews a magic liquid from checkerberries, which, I am told, if you but drink a thimbleful, will enable you to regain your natural shape. There she goes now, over the bridge, on some such errand I dare say."

Ned watched the fairy stepping across the silver network which hung above a miniature Niagara that he could easily have spanned with a single step. Catching up a handful of berries he followed her, not heeding the Gnome's remark "that she would probably prefer to pick them herself," and, almost treading on some of the fairies who were blowing about in the long grass like the flowers they represented, threw the berries in a heap at the door of her castle.

It was, indeed, a most beautiful little palace. Made of brilliant crystals, it sparkled in the sun like a rainbow. Inside, it was even more exquisite, for all her little subjects, the flower fairies and the woodland fays, had adorned it with many lovely things.

Ned stooped over and peeped in at the doorway. There was a bright light inside which came from a little star suspended from the ceiling, the crystal walls on all sides reflecting the light with great brilliancy. Here and there were draped beautiful laces, no doubt spun by the spiders kept by the fairies for that purpose.

"Come," said the Gnome somewhat impatiently, as Ned's curiosity still held him at the little castle's doorway. "Come away, or else the Queen will not return. How is she to enter if you block up her entrance?"

Following his advice, Ned withdrew some little distance and stood watching the gay scene around him.

Hundreds of insects were flying about and large, gay-winged butterflies fluttered over the flowers. On some he noticed tiny figures and others with blades of grass tied around the necks of robins, bluebirds and golden orioles were also flying about in mid-air, while some sailed on the silver backs of fishes or floated in shells upon the water near his feet.

"Look!" cried the Gnome suddenly, "here she comes."

A half horsechestnut, with damask roseleaf cushions, mounted on four ivy-berry wheels and with four shining beetles for horses came driving up from the waterfall.

Leaning back in her carriage sat the Queen Fairy, fanning her face with a fly's wing.

The beetles came to a stand in front of the palace, and the Queen, gathering up her white satin dress, stepped out.

Instantly numerous ladies in waiting, jumped from off their butterfly steeds and escorted her through the palace door.

Ned cautiously peeped in again. The room was filled with fairies about as large as your thumb, dancing here and there and singing a low, sweet song.

On perceiving that a mortal was gazing at them they began to dance more slowly, and presently ceased altogether. Whereupon the Queen, looking about to ascertain the reason and catching sight of Ned's admiring face, exclaimed:

"No wonder you feel so faint, my little fays, and that you stop your merry dancing. The hot air is pouring in upon us from a fiery furnace outside. Look here, my giant friend," she added, coming up to Ned, "if you want to see how we live you mustn't hold your mouth open with astonishment. Your breath is very hot to us little people!"

With that the mischievous Queen jumped quite unexpectedly on Ned's nose and gave it a sharp pinch.

"Don't cry," said the fairy in a cheery voice, the laughs falling from her like waterdrops from the cascade just outside; "I only wanted to let you know what I could do; but I am ready to be as polite as you wish."

"May it please your highness," interposed the Gnome, who at this point squeezed himself through Ned's legs and entered the door, "to give my mortal friend a drop of your crystal nectar, in order that he may regain his boyish shape again?"

The Queen Fairy looked politely inquisitive.

"You see, your highness," the Gnome went on to explain, "he has eaten too heartily of gnome cake, and that together with a gobletful of gnome watermelon juice, has caused him much inconvenience, as well as an entire change of form."

No sooner had he finished speaking than the Queen called the Waterfall Fairy, the Brook Fairy and yet another, somewhat smaller, called Violet Water.

"Hasten," she said to them when they had assembled before her, "hasten to make a draft of crystal nectar, that this mortal may drink and assume once more his natural shape."

"Move off!" cried a shrill voice in Ned's ear, and, looking up, he saw a Snapdragon, who seemed to be a sort of policeman for the fairies.

"How can you expect these Ladies-in-Waiting to fulfill their Queen's commands if you stand there blocking the royal exit?"

"Tell your friend to sit him down and wait patiently, for it will take some time to brew the magic draft," said the Queen to the Gnome, who repeated her words to Ned.

He was very glad indeed to rest, for, not being accustomed to carry so much weight on his young legs, he felt very weary and somewhat discouraged.

However, relief was in sight, and, following the suggestion of the good fairy, he threw himself down on a mossy bank and waited.

Before long the three fairies returned, bearing between them a lily filled with a white liquid.

As they approached the Queen herself came forth from her crystal palace, followed by many of her subjects.

Stepping up to where Ned lay, she said in a soft voice: "Do not rise, for even now you are much too tall. I myself must pour this magic nectar upon your lips."

So saying, she stepped lightly upon a stone close by and, bending forward, placed the lily to Ned's mouth.

"

The next moment he felt a strange sensation running through him, and looking down at his hands and feet was delighted to see that they were becoming smaller and smaller.

Though great was his delight, he did not forget his manners, and, turning to the little fairy, said: "How may I ever repay you for your great kindness? Indeed," he added, scarcely able to restrain the tears which came to his eyes, "whatever would my dear mother have thought had I returned to her in the form of a giant?"

"Thank me no more," answered the Fairy Queen, "for gladly will I do any favor for the boy who thinks of his mother first. In the future, should you need my aid, hang this ring about a bluebird's throat and send him to me."

And with these words she placed a slender gold ring upon Ned's little finger.

"But how shall I catch the bird?" asked Ned, his curiosity aroused before he had time to think of thanking her small highness.

"Whistle thrice upon a blade of grass," she answered, "and the bird will fly to thee. Then place the ring about his neck and bid him hasten to the Fairy Queen of the Lake."

During all this time Ned had been growing smaller and smaller. He had almost forgotten this, when his little friend, the Gnome, exclaimed: "There! You're your own self again!" At which Ned turned to the Queen, and, after thanking her again ran hastily to the brook to assure himself that such was the case.

So, bidding farewell to his kind friend, the Fairy Queen, and her three Ladies-in-Waiting, he accompanied the Gnome down the valley.

THE MAGIC AXE

PRESENTLY the Gnome turned to Ned and said:

"I must leave you for a time. But with the Fairy Queen's magic ring upon your finger, you will be safe from harm. Self reliance is what all boys should practise. Therefore, travel for a few days alone. At the end of that time I will join you." And with these words the Gnome disappeared.

For a moment Ned felt a wild desire to call him back. But with a shrug of his shoulder, he put away the thought and bravely set out in search of further adventure.

He had gone but a short distance when he came to a Magic Axe, chopping away all by itself at one of the tallest trees.

"Good morning, Mistress Axe," he said. "Doesn't it tire you to be chopping away all alone there at that old tree?"

"Not at all, my son. Put me in your knapsack and I will make you famous."

Picking up the axe, Ned placed it in his knapsack and set off once more. After a while, he came to a place where the road was hollowed out of a mass of solid rock, and here, in the distance, he heard a sharp noise like that of iron striking against stone.

"Some giant must be breaking rocks away up there," he said to himself, and climbed up the mountain. When he reached the top of the high rock, he found a Magic Pickaxe, all alone by itself, digging away at the hard stone as if it were soft clay.

Every time that wonderful pickaxe struck a blow it went more than a foot into the rock.

"Good morning, Mistress Pickaxe," said Ned. "Doesn't it tire you to be digging alone here, hollowing away at that old rock?"

"Not at all, my little man. Put me in your knapsack and I will make you famous."

Ned picked up the pickaxe and placing it in his knapsack, again went on.

After a while he came to a brook which he followed up the hillside.

The farther he went the smaller it grew until finally, it ended in a little nutshell, from which this tiny stream began its journey down the mountain.

"Good morning, Miss Spring," said Ned. "Doesn't it tire you to be gushing away all alone by yourself in your little corner?"

"Indeed it does, my little man. Put me in your knapsack and I will make you famous."

Ned picked up the little nutshell and plugging it up with moss, placed it carefully in his knapsack with the Magic Axe and the Magic Pickaxe.

After some little time he came to a king's palace. Now, although it was a magnificent palace, everyone living there was perfectly miserable, for one morning, without the least warning, an immense oak had sprung up, with leaves and branches so thick that they shut out the sun from all the windows, making the castle as dark as night.

Of course in those days there was no gas and electricity, and although the king had commanded that candles be made as high as barber poles, they spluttered and often went out when the wind blew.

All the woodcutters in the kingdom had tried to cut down this tree, but its bark was so tough that it turned the edge of every axe, and for every branch that was lopped off, two instantly grew in its place. At last the king had offered three bags of gold to anyone who would rid him of his troublesome oaktree.

Now this was not the only trouble that beset the poor king. For, although the surrounding country was rich in springs and brooks, the royal gardens were dry as the desert of Sahara. And although the king had also promised three bags of gold to anyone who would dig a well, no one had yet been able to dig deeper than a foot, as the palace was built on a rock of solid granite.

Each day the king grew more angry, but of course that did no good. At last calling the poet laureate of his kingdom, he asked him what should be done.

Running his fingers through his long curly hair, the poet thought a while. Then summoning the Royal Carpenter, ordered him to make an immense placard, on which, when finished, this wise poet printed:

"To him who cuts my oaktree down

I'll give three bags of gold

But he who fails shall lose his life

And lie beneath the mold."

"But what good will that exquisite poem do?" asked the king, sarcastically.

"It will keep your Royal Highness from being irritated by this endless sound of chop, chop, chop," replied the poet. "I verily believe every man in your kingdom has had a hack at the tree. Now, he who reads this sign, will first make sure his axe is a good one. And my poetic ears will be spared much of this frightful noise which is far worse than a steel rivetter at work on a ninety story building in New York City." Which shows that this poet had an eye that could see into the future, for at that time, as far as I know, Columbus hadn't even asked the Queen of Spain to pawn her diamond rings!

"Very well," replied the king, "have the sign nailed on this dreadful tree and we will see what happens."

As soon as Ned arrived at the castle he bowed politely to the king, who happened to be standing nearby with all his courtiers.

"Ha, ha," laughed the king, as Ned read the sign. "Do you, too, wish to lose your ears?" At which all the courtiers laughed heartily, the first time in many months that anybody in that castle had laughed, or even smiled, for that matter.

"I can but try," answered Ned bravely, and opening his knapsack, took out his Magic Axe. Standing it up, with the handle leaning against the enchanted tree, he stepped back a few feet and shouted: "Chop, chop, chop!"

At once the axe began to chop, now right, now left, and up and down, and in an incredibly short time that immense tree was cut to bits. It took only a quarter of an hour, and yet there was such a monstrous heap of wood that the whole court needed nothing else to burn for a whole year.

But when Ned asked the king for the three bags of gold, that stingy old monarch said, "Before I give you the reward, you must perform another task."

"What is it?" asked Ned.

"You must dig me a well so that I may have plenty of water," answered the king.

THE MAGIC SPRING

"I CAN but try, your Majesty," said Ned bravely, and again opening his knapsack, took out his Magic Pickaxe. Laying it carefully on the ground in the proper position, he shouted:

"Pick, pick, pick!"

At once the pick began to burst the granite to splinters, and in less than a quarter of an hour had dug a well more than a hundred feet deep in the solid rock.

"Is the well deep enough, your Majesty?" asked Ned politely.

"Certainly," answered the king, "but where is the water to come from?" And he winked at his courtiers, who smiled to themselves, for they all thought Ned would fail, after all, for as yet there wasn't a drop of water in the well.

But Ned wasn't discouraged. He quietly opened his knapsack again and took out the nutshell covered with moss, and placed it on a magnificent fountain vase which, not having any water, had been filled with a beautiful bouquet of flowers.

"Gush, gush, gush!" he shouted, stepping aside to avoid a wetting.

At once water began to burst out among the flowers, singing with a gentle murmur, and falling down in a sparkling cascade, that was so cold it made everybody shiver. And in less than a quarter of an hour the well was filled, and a deep trench had to be dug to take away the overflow, otherwise the whole palace would have been flooded.

"You have indeed earned the reward," said the king. And he ordered a little donkey saddled and bridled and the six bags of gold hung from his back, three on either side. After which Ned was invited to a great feast, and when that was over, he mounted the little donkey and rode away, with the three bags of gold hanging from each side of the saddle and a little gold ring on his finger, which the king's daughter gave him after washing her pretty face in water for the first time in many months.

But before Ned rode away, he put his Magic Axe and his Magic Pickaxe back in his knapsack, "for who can tell," he said to himself, "what need I may have of these two useful tools."

His knapsack was now well filled, for the cook in the royal kitchen had also placed in it a loaf of bread, a cheese and a knife in case he became hungry while on his journey of adventure.

As Ned traveled on, the forest became darker and darker, for the trees grew so close together that the sun could hardly shine through the thick leafy roof. Suddenly he heard a great voice singing:

"I am the master of this wood

And everyone bows to me,

My head is as big as a drygoods box

And my legs as long as a tree."

Then, all at once, the voice changed to a whistle, which sounded like the siren on a sound steamer when the weather is foggy.

"It must be a giant singing," thought Ned. "Goodness! but he's a loud whistler. I guess he blows through his fingers!" and he hid beneath a clump of bushes.

"Ho, ho!" cried the voice, and a giant came crashing through the forest.

On seeing Ned, he shouted:

"Come out of there, and I'll make a mouthful of you."

"Don't be in a hurry," replied Ned bravely. "I'm going to make you my servant."

"Ho, ho!" laughed the giant, "that is a good joke! I'll pitch you into that raven's nest up there to teach you to make less noise in my forest."

"Your forest!" laughed Ned. "It's as much mine as yours, and if you say another word, I'll cut it down in a quarter of an hour."

"Ha, ha!" shouted the giant, "I should like to see you begin, my brave Sir Kid!"

Carefully placing his Magic Axe on the ground, Ned shouted, "Chop, chop, chop!"

At once the axe began to chop, now right, now left, and up and down, till the branches tumbled down on the giant's head like hail in autumn.

"Stop, stop!" cried the giant. "Don't destroy my forest. Who the mischief are you?"

"Sit down and I'll tell you the story of the famous Puss in Boots, who once killed a giant and gave his castle to his Master, the Lord of Carabas," said Ned.

"How could a cat kill a giant? You are making sport of me."

"Not at all," replied Ned. "Have you never read the story of Puss in Boots?"

"No, but I once heard my cousin, the Giant of the Beanstalk, speak of a cat who wore boots. But that was long ago when we were both boys."

"Well, I'll tell you then," said Ned. "Puss in Boots' master was the youngest of three sons. When their father died, the two older brothers received the farm and money, while he was left nothing but a Cat, who said to him one day, 'Do just what I tell you and I will make you rich. Give me a bag and a pair of boots, because the brambles scratch my legs, and you shall see what I will do for you.'

"Well, when the boots were made and he had put them on, he hung the bag about his neck, and set out for a rabbit warren where lived great numbers of rabbits. Opening the bag he stretched himself out as though he were dead, and waited for a hungry rabbit to poke his nose into the bag to eat the bran. Pretty soon along came a young rabbit and as soon as it had crept in to eat the bran, Puss in Boots pulled the string, and that was the last of the little rabbit.

"Then, running off to the palace, he gave it to the king, saying it was a present from his master, my Lord of Carabas, the name he had invented for his young master. Every day he brought some kind of game, until by and by the king thought my Lord of Carabas a great man and Puss in Boots a most wonderful cat, which indeed he was."

"He was indeed," said the big giant, moving uneasily on the log on which he was sitting.

"Well, one day," continued Ned, "Puss in Boots bade his master bathe in the river, and leave the rest to him. Just then the King passed by.

"'Help, help!' cried Puss. 'Robbers have stolen my master's clothes!'

"At once the king ordered his guards to the rescue, and fitting out my Lord of Carabas with a new suit of clothes, invited him to ride in the coach with his beautiful daughter.

"As they rolled along they came in sight of a castle owned by a bad giant."

MAGIC FOOD

"PUSS IN BOOTS, who had reached the castle in advance of the royal party, opened the door and said with a low bow to the wicked ogre:

"'I hear you have the power to change yourself into any animal.'

"'That is true,' answered the ogre, so pleased that at once he turned himself into a lion.

"'I doubt if you can become as small as a mouse,' said Puss in Boots.

"Instantly the ogre changed himself into a mouse, whereupon Puss in Boots pounced upon him and ate him up.

"At that moment up drove the coach. Throwing open the castle door, Puss in Boots said with a hospitable bow:

"'Welcome to the castle of my Lord of Carabas.' And, to make a long story short," laughed Ned, "his master married the King's daughter and lived happily ever after."

"Whew!" gasped the giant. "He certainly was a wonderful cat," and he looked anxiously at the Magic Axe.

Presently Ned began to feel hungry, and opening his knapsack, took out his bread and cheese.

"What is that white stuff?" asked the giant, who had never seen cheese before.

"That is a stone," answered Ned, commencing to eat it with a hungry appetite.

"Do you eat stones?" asked the giant.

"Oh yes," answered Ned. "That's my regular food, which explains why I'm not so big as you who eat oxen; but it's also the reason why, little as I am, I am ten times as strong as you are. Now take me to your house."

The giant looked at the Magic Axe which had so nearly destroyed his forest, and then at Ned eating a stone with apparent relish.

"I will," he said, and humbly led the way to his monstrous cabin.

"Now listen," said Ned to the giant after they were fairly seated, "one of us must be the master, and the other the servant. If I can't do whatever you do, I am to be your slave; if you're not able to do whatever I do, you are to be mine."

"Agreed," said the giant. "I'd be tickled to death to have a little servant like you. It's too much work for me to think, and you have brains enough for both. Well, let's start the trial. Here are my two buckets,—go and get the water to make the soup!"

Ned looked at the buckets, the tops of which he couldn't even see, for they were two enormous hogsheads, ten feet high and six broad. It would have been much easier for him to drown himself in them than to move them.

"Ho, ho!" shouted the giant. "Do what I do and get the water."

"What's the good of that?" replied Ned. "I'll go get the spring itself to put in the pot," knowing that he could easily run back to the king's castle for the little magic nutshell.

"No, no!" said the giant, "that won't do. You have already half spoiled my forest with your Magic Axe. I don't want you to take my spring away. You may attend to the fire, and I'll go for the water."

So the giant hung up the kettle, put into it an ox cut into pieces, fifty cabbages, and a wagon-load of carrots, skimming the broth with a frying pan, tasting it every now and then until it was done. When everything was ready, he turned and said:

"Now we'll see if you can do what I can. I feel like eating the whole ox, and you into the bargain. I think I'll serve you for dessert."

"All right," answered little Ned. But before sitting down he slipped his knapsack under his jacket.

Then the two champions set to work. Perhaps Ned was a trifle nervous, knowing only too well that if he failed he must be the giant's servant.

Well, the giant ate and ate, and Ned wasn't idle; only he pitched everything, beef, cabbage, carrots, and all, into his knapsack when the giant wasn't looking.

"Ouf!" at last grunted the giant, "I can't do much more. I've got to undo the lower button of my waistcoat."

"Eat away, starveling!" cried Ned, sticking half a cabbage into his knapsack.

"Ouf!" groaned the giant, "I must loosen another button. But what sort of an ostrich's stomach have you got, Kiddo? I should say you were used to eating stones!"

"Eat away, lazy-bones!" said Ned, sticking a huge chunk of beef into his knapsack.

"Ouf!" sighed the giant for the third time, "I must open the third button."

"Bah!" answered Ned. "It's the easiest thing to relieve yourself," and taking his knife, he slit his jacket and the knapsack under it the whole length of his stomach. "Now's your turn. Do as I do, if you can!"

"Excuse me!" gasped the giant. "You win. I'd rather be your servant than do that."

Then kissing Ned's hand in token of submission, he lifted his little master on his shoulder, and slinging the six bags of gold over his back, started off through the forest.

"Wait a minute," said Ned, "I've forgotten my Magic tools." So the giant picked them up and thrusting them in his pocket, again set off at a tremendous rate.

After a while, they came in sight of a great castle where lived a lord even more wicked than the cruel Blue Beard. As they drew nearer, they heard loud screams like those of some fair lady in distress. The next minute the wicked lord dragged a lovely lady by the hair across the courtyard.

With one stride the giant stepped over the castle wall.

"Shall I toss him over the moon?" he asked.

"No, leave him to me," replied Ned. The wicked lord trembled and grew as pale as a white swan that swam nearby in a beautiful fountain.

"My giant servant at a sign from me, will pitch you over the moon. But instead, as you have the reputation of being the greatest liar that ever lived, we will see who can tell the biggest story, you or I. If you lose, you shall give your castle to this fair lady and take yourself off, I don't care where, but you must never return."

At once the wicked lord commenced to tell the biggest story he could imagine.

"I have a bull so large that a man can sit on each of his horns, and the two can't touch each other with a twenty foot pole."

"Oh, that's nothing," replied Ned. "At home on the farm we have a bull so large that a servant sitting on one of his horns can't see the servant sitting on the other."

"You win," laughed the pretty princess, clapping her hands at Ned. Then the wicked lord went to his stable and saddling his best horse, rode away. But as he passed through the gate, Ned touched his steed with his magic gold ring. Instantly the horse turned into an immense bird and flew away. But where he went no one knows to this day.

MAGIC EARS

"DEAR me," said the giant suddenly. "I've forgotten all about my errand. You and your Magic Axe have robbed me of my memory," and the big man scratched his hand and looked anxiously at Ned.

"What is it?"

"I was to take a chicken to my old mother," answered the giant sadly.

"Go ahead," said Ned. "I can take care of myself. At any rate it is about time my friend the Gnome came back to me."

"You are very kind," said the giant. "Here are your Magic Axe and your Magic Pickaxe. I almost forgot them," and he set off at a great rate for his mother's house.

Ned, too, quickened his pace, for it was growing late, and the shadows creeping from tree to tree. At length he saw a light in the distance. It was a very little light, not much larger than a star, and at first Ned thought it might be a giant firefly. However, he kept on and after a while it turned out to be a little candle in the window of a poor woodcutter's hut. Knocking on the door, it was presently opened by a strange looking man. He had long hairy ears like a donkey and was dressed in the skins of wild animals.

"Welcome," he said in a kindly voice, "I am just preparing my evening meal. Come in and eat." Ned followed the donkey-eared man into the cottage and sat down at the rude wooden table on which were spread black bread and beans.

"I have but humble fare to offer you," said the donkey-eared man, but his smile was a kind one as he helped Ned to the beans with a large wooden spoon. "But as I see you are a traveler, you no doubt have fared worse at times," and he smiled again in such a friendly way, that Ned took a great liking to him.

"You are right. I'm a traveler, seeking adventures and many strange things I have seen while visiting Gnomeland."

"I have heard little of the world since my ears were changed into those of a donkey," sighed the donkey-eared man.

"Is there no magic charm which will remove them?" asked Ned, as he finished the last bean on his plate and wiped his mouth carefully with the pocket handkerchief which his kind mother had given him the very morning he had set out for Gnomeland.

"None whatever," answered the man with a sigh. "There is no charm nor magic herb, but I've heard tell of a Magic Axe that once cut down a charmed oak tree overshadowing a king's palace. But where am I to find that Magic Axe?"

"Oh master dear, pray ask this lad

Your donkey ears to sever;

For then your own two ears will take

Their place as good as ever,"

sang a little bird from her tree in the forest.

When Ned heard that, he jumped up and went behind the door where he had hung his knapsack. Taking out the Magic Axe, he laid it on the table before the donkey-eared man.

"Cut off my ears!" shouted the donkey-eared man.

"I can't do it," said Ned, trembling all over.

"Do as I ask you," begged the donkey-eared man, laying his head on the table.

Instead, however, Ned touched the donkey ears with his little magic gold ring, at the same time whispering, "Away with you!"

Off went the long, hairy ears, and the next minute, two grew in their place, just like yours and mine.

"Oh, now I'm free from donkey ears,

Three cheers and once, again, three cheers!

No more the witch's evil snare

Shall force me donkey ears to wear!"

sang the donkey-eared man, dancing about the room.

All the next day Ned trudged on alone until towards evening, he came to the edge of a pine-forest, where close at hand stood a small hut made of pine-branches, plastered with mud and thatched with rye-straw. No sooner had he tapped on the door than it was opened by a girl. She looked out timidly, thinking, I suppose, it might be a robber. But when she saw Ned, she smiled.

"Come in," she said, and Ned saw four small children staring curiously at him.

The room was very smoky, for there was no chimney to the rude hut. A hole in the roof let the smoke out, and there were no windows, for the father of these children was a poor peasant who made his living by gathering turpentine in the pine forest.

Ned sat down, while the girl went on with her work until the black beans were ready for supper, when she put them all in a big wooden bowl, and invited Ned to join her and the four children.

While they were eating out of the bowl with a wooden spoon, a tame jackdaw who had been sitting on an old stool by the fireside, hopped over and perched himself close to Ned.

When the supper was over, and the children were ready for bed, he whispered, "This little family is very poor. Their father is away selling turpentine, and there is little food in the cupboard. But if you will come with me tonight, I will show you how we can help them."

When all the children were sound asleep, Ned looked over to the fireside where the jackdaw sat, his eyes shining brighter and brighter through the darkness, till they made the room so light that Ned could plainly see the five sleeping children huddled together on the straw bed in the corner.

Then the jackdaw nodded, and hopping down from the stool on which he sat, walked softly over to the door.

The moon shone brightly on the bare brown fields silvered with white frost, and in the still, cold air, the forest looked like a black cloud just dropped upon the earth.

THE MAGIC BASKET

ON and on they went, the jackdaw hopping over the rough fields, and now and then turning his head and winking his fiery eyes at Ned, until they found themselves at the foot of a high, round hill.

At one side of the great mound the stream which they had been following suddenly stopped short, making a deep well, over which hung an old oak tree, leafless now, but still strewing the ground with dry acorns.

Right at the foot of this tree was an upright gray stone, apparently part of a rock deeply sunk in the hillside. Beside this stone the jackdaw paused, and, turning to nod reassuringly at Ned, picked up a pebble about the size of an acorn and dropped it into the well, at the same time knocking gently on the flat stone with his bill.

In a moment the rock opened in the middle, and there stood a little old woman, as withered as a spring apple and as bright as a butterfly, dressed in a scarlet bodice covered with spangles and a black petticoat worked in square characters with all the colors of the rainbow.

Ned thought she was not nearly as attractive as the fairies whom he had but lately left, although she had on more colors than even the Queen Fairy.

On seeing the jackdaw she made a low bow, and in a shrill eager voice invited them in. Ned hesitated, but the little old woman snatched his hand and pulled him in, asking in a whisper, "Dost thou fear for thyself when visiting the King of the Gnomes?"

Then, opening a low door in the side of the cavern, she beckoned them to follow. In the middle of a still larger vault stood an arm chair fashioned from beryl and jasper, with knobs of amethyst and topaz, in which sat Ned's friend, the Gnome.

He was dressed in a robe of velvet, green and soft as forest moss, and a ring of gold lay on his grizzled hair. His little eyes shone keen and fiery, and his hands, withered and brown, were now covered with glittering jewels.

About the cave a hundred little men, smaller than he, were busy in a hundred ways. Some stirred kettles of smoking broth; others sliced fresh vegetables for crisp salads. Some spread a table, with golden plates and crystal goblets; three turned huge pieces of meat on a spit before a fire at the end of the cavern, while a dozen more watched the simmering pots.

The jackdaw hopped gravely past all this toward the chair of the Gnome King, who stretched out his sceptre, a tall bulrush of gold, and touched the jackdaw, who at once turned into a dwarf.

Making a low bow to the Gnome King, he turned to Ned and said:

"I was forced to take the form of a jackdaw for twenty years because I once said that gold was not as yellow as buttercups nor so bright as sunshine. This made the Gnomes angry, because their belief is that gold is the most beautiful thing in the world. My punishment is now over and I need never return to the earth again. But I would do a favor to the poor peasant children who were so good to me."

"What favor would you ask for the poor peasant children?" asked the Gnome King.

"I would send them a Magic Basket filled with food," answered the dwarf.

No sooner had he spoken, than the Gnome ordered his subjects to fill a Magic Basket with all kinds of good things to eat. There was a golden bowl of smoking stew, a crystal goblet of wine, a golden dish of mashed potatoes and another of rice pudding.

And when the Magic Basket was covered with a damask napkin, it was handed to a dwarf messenger to take to the poor woodcutter's children, while all the little dwarfs stood around him and sang:

"In this basket they will find

Food and drink of magic kind.

Never will it empty grow

And no hunger they shall know."

"Hereafter," said the Gnome King, looking kindly at Ned, "a bluebird shall be your companion and will show you many and curious things. I can spare no more time, for my people must be governed, and while I have given you more attention than any other mortal because of your great fondness for fairy tales, I must now leave you in the care of this bluebird, unless, perchance, you wish to return to earth at once."

To which Ned answered eagerly that he would much rather see more of Gnomeland before again returning to the everyday routine of grammar school and lessons.

"Good luck to you, then!" cried his friend, as he shook Ned warmly by the hand.

The door opened and Ned once more found himself by the side of the great flat stone in the hillside, where rippling waters of the little stream flowed into the pool at the foot of the great oak tree, on which sat a lovely bluebird.

Following the bluebird, Ned turned to one side to avoid climbing the hill, and continued his journey for some time, keeping ever in sight the bluebird's beautiful form.

It was almost dark when they were confronted by a dense forest. This was not particularly reassuring to Ned, especially as the bluebird flew back and settled herself on his shoulder, evidently not wishing to enter the woods at so late an hour. For in a deep, black forest, with all sorts of strange shadows and ghostly trees, one never knows what may be lurking about, and the same Ned who, with his two stout fists, in broad daylight would have undertaken to keep any living boy or man from doing serious mischief, felt his teeth set hard and his heart stand still as he came into the shadow of the great trees.

The little bird nestled close to his cheek and refused to leave his shoulder.

Ned, indeed, felt that he must now look out for himself, and though his heart beat high, he bravely trudged forward.

It was very unlike the woods to which he had been accustomed to go with his schoolmates at home, where bright green maples, beeches and birches made a leafy bower overhead. Instead, there were solemn pines and hemlocks, and as he entered deeper, great caverns appeared in the rocks and narrow gulleys, into which one might easily fall and break one's neck.

Through this dismal place he trudged along, with his knees shaking, but with a brave heart, until he came to a great pine, which evidently had been struck by lightning, for it stood up white and tall, lifting its bare arms to the sky, like some specter giant crying for vengeance.

Luckily he had placed the bluebird in his pocket, fearing that the low hanging branches would sweep it from his shoulders. Had he not done so before arriving at this spot the opportunity would not have presented itself again.

Right at the foot of the pine, on a decaying log, sat a little old man, who was altogether the ugliest looking object that Ned had ever seen. He was about half the size of ordinary men, though the whiteness of his hair and beard showed plainly that he would never be any taller, and though his body was short and crooked to the last degree, his face was long and pale, but was lighted up by wonderfully brilliant eyes.

These were fixed on Ned from the moment he came in sight, and, piercing through the darkness, it is no wonder that they chilled the poor boy's blood and failed to quicken his pace. Indeed, it is not quite certain that he would have gone forward at all if the greater part of the forest had not been behind him, though there seemed to be a spell in the strange eyes that drew the boy on in spite of himself.

"Come along! What are you afraid of?" cried the dwarf in a little, dry voice, that sounded like the cracking of a dry twig beneath one's foot.

Ned hesitated, and, as if seeking the comfort of something alive and friendly, thrust his hand into his pocket alongside of the little bluebird.

"Come on! Come on, little master," repeated the dwarf. "Here I have been waiting more than an hour to tell you some good news, and now that you are here you would hinder me because you are such a coward."

"I don't know you," said Ned, as an excuse.

"Well, well, no matter for that. I know you well enough. Would you read about gnomes and then be so cowardly that you would fear to associate with them?"

As he finished speaking, he arose, disclosing a doorway in the trunk of the pine tree behind him.

At that moment, a beautiful dwarf maiden emerged therefrom, and, as if having heard the conversation, said: "He is no coward, father. See, he will shake hands with me!"

Ned put out his hand, but drew it back just in time to escape having the gold ring which the Fairy Queen had given him, slipped off his finger by the dwarf maiden.

"Selfish mortal," she cried, "'tis nothing but a little gold band. Give it to me. See, I will exchange this beautiful diamond for it," and she held out a sparkling stone set in a gold ring.

Ned drew back in alarm, more especially as the dwarf himself advanced with a threatening attitude.

Continuing to step back, Ned kept his eyes upon the dwarf, who advanced now with upraised fist. Seeing this, Ned quickly threw off his coat and picking up a stout stick, prepared to defend himself.

It would have gone ill with him, for the dwarf was surprisingly strong and agile, had not relief come from an unexpected quarter.

The little bluebird had quietly slipped out of Ned's pocket, and flying up to him, received the gold ring about her neck in accordance with the command of the Fairy Queen, which Ned remembered suddenly and luckily in time.

Off flew the bird to the great tall pine and touched it with the magic ring. In an instant it changed into a giant, who stretched forth one of his great hands, and catching up the dwarf, hurled him headlong down the side of the ravine close by.

The dwarf maiden, with a cry, rushed after him, climbing down the sides with wonderful agility.

The giant now turned to Ned, saying: "Little Master, I owe it to you that I am once more my natural self. An evil spirit transformed me into yonder tree, but the magic of your ring has restored me once more to my natural shape. I will henceforth serve you while the occasion lasts," and with these words he knelt before Ned most humbly.

At the same time the bluebird handed Ned his magic ring, and with this faithful little friend, his gold ring, and the giant for a servant, Ned felt that he had nothing further to fear while traveling in Gnomeland.

"Thank you, my good friend," said Ned, placing his hand upon the bowed head of the giant. "You are certainly grateful for what I have done for you, which is more than can be said of many mortals. But had I not had the magic ring and the assistance of my little companion, the bluebird, you would still be the tree you were. Let us, therefore, the three of us, pledge allegiance to one another and set out upon our journey of adventure."

As he finished speaking the giant arose and carefully placing Ned upon his shoulder, started off at a rapid stride.

The little bluebird flew ahead, and in a short time the three comrades emerged from the forest.

In the distance could be seen the turrets of a stately castle, which looked down from a high point of land upon a beautiful river that wound in and out like a silver ribbon through the meadow.

"Who lives in yonder castle?" asked Ned, unconsciously adopting the style of language of Gnomeland.

"I know not," answered the giant, "but with a few more steps we will be able to inquire at the postern gates."

It was indeed a stately castle, and upon reaching the drawbridge Ned was surprised to find that it was not lowered for them to cross over, although they waited for some time.

"I think I'll blow upon my policeman's whistle," said Ned, hunting through his pockets. "I certainly had it when I left home."

"Blow hard," advised the giant as Ned brought it forth, "blow hard, that those within may think us worthy of admittance."

Upon which Ned let out a blast that would do justice to any Knight of the Round Table. He was himself surprised at the volume of sound, but was too much interested in what was about to happen to realize that the touch of his magic ring had made it possible for the small nickel-plated whistle to create such a sound.

Presently the drawbridge began slowly to descend, and when the creaking chains ceased their noise, our three comrades crossed over to the castle gates. These were thrown wide open, and just as the giant placed Ned upon his feet in front of the castle doors, they opened, disclosing a beautiful princess on the threshold.

"Welcome, Ned, to you and your two friends."

Whereupon the giant bowed very low, and the little bluebird flew over and nestled on her shoulder.

Ned was too delighted to speak for a moment, for up to this time his experiences had been most trying, but here at last it seemed that fortune smiled upon him.

So he and the giant followed her into the stately hall, the latter finding it necessary to stoop each time he entered a doorway, for although the castle was built on magnificent lines it had not occurred to the architect that a giant would ever be a guest.

When they were all seated, except the giant, who sprawled on the floor, as there was no chair large enough to accommodate him, the beautiful princess said:

"I would ask you to spend the night here, but my wicked stepfather returns tonight, and I fear he will do you some injury."

"I fear nothing," answered Ned courageously, standing up to appear more dignified, "and if I can be of any service to you, say but a word, for I have a trusty friend in the giant, and also a clever one in my little bluebird, to say nothing of the magic of this ring," and he touched the gold band about his finger and bowed again to the beautiful princess.

"My stepfather is very crafty," said the princess, looking at Ned intently, as if weighing the possibilities of his assistance. "He once changed a giant into a pine tree!" At these words, the giant began to shake and tremble so that the cut glass chandeliers rattled all over the castle.

"Remember, I have the magic ring," Ned whispered, leaning over to where the giant lay upon the floor; "nothing can harm us with that in our possession."

"What would you have me do?" asked Ned, turning again to the beautiful princess, for he felt that she was unwilling to ask him the favor, fearing it might prove of harm to him.

Still the beautiful princess remained silent until the bluebird began to sing a sweet song, perching meanwhile upon her shoulder, as if intending the song for her ears especially.

Then tears fell from her eyes.

"'Tis the song my brother was wont to sing," she said, "but now"—and hiding her face in her hands, she wept more bitterly than before—"he has been sent away and hidden by my cruel stepfather I know not where."

"We will find him for you, princess," cried Ned. "Fear not, for I have confidence in my two comrades and in myself. Give us all something to eat that we may have strength to undertake this adventure."

The princess immediately ordered a great feast to be set before them, and when our three comrades had eaten their fill they once more set out upon their journey, with the prayers of the beautiful princess for their safety and successful return.

As they wound their way through the pleasant valley, every so often the little bluebird would sing her song, loud and sweet, and then would pause, with folded wing, to listen, as if expecting an answer.

So they went on for many miles, until, as they approached a cottage by the roadside, Ned thought he heard a familiar air. Indeed, he was sure that something important was about to happen, for the bluebird was whirring around in circles and singing as if her life depended upon the way she trilled and warbled.

"Why, there is a bluebird in that wicker cage!" exclaimed Ned, pointing toward the cottage porch, from which swung a bird cage.

It was, indeed, true, and in another moment Ned's bluebird was perched on the railing close by.

Scrambling down from the giant's friendly shoulder, Ned touched the cage, and, to his amazement, the little door flew open and out walked a handsome young prince, about his own age.
"Who are you?" cried Ned, but before he could reply the giant exclaimed: "He must be the brother of the princess! We have, indeed, completed our adventure, or nearly so," he added, remembering they had yet to deal with the crafty stepfather.
"How can I ever repay you?" cried the little prince, who was at first unable to speak from the joy of it all. "I am free! I am free!" And he almost cried with delight, flinging his arms about Ned's sturdy form and patting the leg of the giant.
"Come, little bluebird, and let me thank you, too," he added, as the pretty bird circled in the air and alighted on Ned's shoulder. Indeed, it was a happy moment for all.
"And now," said Ned, "let us think of the best way to return to the castle, so that the princess may receive her long-lost brother."
"The easiest way is the best way," said the giant. "Both you boys climb up on my back, and in 500 short seconds we'll be back at the castle, or I have forgotten my early training on the cinder path."
All of which goes to show that even in Gnomeland there are sports, although few fairy tales tell us anything about them.
When Ned and the prince had seated themselves comfortably on the great shoulders of the obliging giant, he set off at a tremendous rate, and soon they were ascending the hill on which stood the castle of the beautiful princess.

THE MAGIC RING

NED followed the beautiful princess and her brother into the castle, while the giant, who had to stoop nearly to the floor in order to enter the doorway, brought up the rear.

As it was late, everyone decided to go to bed. Besides, they were all well tired out after their exciting day.

You would have laughed to see the giant ascend the stairway to the royal bedchambers, for the steps were too small for his feet, and it was with great difficulty that he managed to get a foothold with the toes of his boots.

When at last he was safely inside his bedroom, the largest in the castle, it was found that the bedstead was not nearly long enough for him.

So the princess gave orders that two cot beds be placed ends together, and in this way the giant, by allowing his feet to project through the open window, could lie down at full length. His feet nearly reached the tree that grew just outside, on which the little bluebird had perched for the night, and it was lucky, indeed, that it was midsummer, for otherwise our big friend might have caught a severe cold.

After bidding the giant goodnight the little bluebird had a few minutes' talk with Ned while he undressed himself.

She agreed to act as sentinel during the night, to keep a vigilant lookout from the treetop, and in case of approaching danger instantly to awaken Ned and the giant.

Gradually the great castle grew quiet, until nothing was stirring, "not even a mouse."

At times the night wind rustled the leaves in the tree where the little bluebird sentinel sat winking and blinking, and the big yellow moon glistened fantastically on the big toe of the giant.

Toward midnight a faint sound in the distance, like the beat of horses' hoofs, startled the bluebird.

Hastily flying toward the castle entrance she gazed out upon the roadway that wound up from the valley below.

At some distance she made out dimly the figures of a number of horsemen.

Returning swiftly to the castle, she tweaked the giant's big toe. That, you can easily imagine, awoke him with a start.

"What's the matter?" he asked in a frightened whisper which, although only a whisper, was enough to make the castle tremble, thereby awakening Ned and the princess herself.

"The crafty stepfather of the princess is coming," answered the bluebird.

"Then it's all up with me," cried the giant, "for he'll change me again into a pine tree."

The bluebird made no reply, but hastened to find Ned. On entering his bedroom through the half open window she found him already dressing. "Take the ring," he said, slipping it over her glossy neck, after she had informed him of what she had seen. "If you can manage to touch him with it, this wicked man will find that he has no power whatever to harm us."

"I will make haste," replied the little bird, "for they must by this time have reached the drawbridge."

So saying she flew swiftly away and reached the other side of the moat just as the cavalcade set foot upon the bridge.

Awaiting her opportunity to touch the wicked stepfather of the princess with the magic ring, she alighted quietly on the tip of a spear which one of the horsemen carried.

As they neared the center of the drawbridge the king, as if suddenly aware of an unseen power, exclaimed: "I feel there is danger near!"

Then the horseman shook his spear defiantly and so startled the little bluebird that she nearly lost her footing, and alas! what was much more serious, caused her to loosen her hold upon the little magic gold ring, which slipped from between her bill and fell into the waters of the moat.

Like a falling star, it shivered and glimmered in the rays of the moon as it descended, attracting the attention of a speckled trout, who opened his mouth and swallowed it as it splashed upon the silvery surface of the water.

"Your trusty spear has done me good service in times gone by," exclaimed the wicked king, not knowing that its owner had unknowingly been the cause of saving him at the present moment.

On came the cavalcade, the wicked attendants of the king inside the castle opening the gates and allowing him and his men to enter the courtyard.

Ned looked down from his window and wondered what had become of the bluebird. He did not feel afraid, but at the same time he realized that he was not in friendly hands. The giant, on hearing the gates open, had quickly drawn in his feet and was struggling to get his shoes on when Ned appeared at the door.

"It's all up!" said the big fellow, with a wry face and a catch in his gruff voice. "I can feel already the pine-needles beginning to stick out all over me."

"Oh, that's gooseflesh, you're so scared!" replied Ned, smiling in spite of the gravity of the situation. "It may not be as bad as you think!"

Just then a great pounding on the front doors told them that the King was seeking admittance. "Who has locked the doors?" he shouted.

"Wait a minute," said the sweet voice of the princess; "we did not expect you so late," and she ran down the stairs and opened the door herself.

"I have two visitors upstairs," she said, as the angry monarch stepped inside.

"What!" he shouted hoarsely, "bring them to me. How do I know but that they are enemies?"

"Indeed they are not," she replied, "as you will see in 500 short seconds."

"Ned, come down!" she called, "bring your friend with you, for I would have you meet the King!"

Ned turned to the giant, whose big face was twitching with terror. "He'll recognize me as sure as eggs is eggs!" he groaned.

"What! is that thunder?" exclaimed the King below, mistaking the giant's moan for a thunderclap, but before his question was answered Ned and his friend appeared at the head of the stairway.

After shaking hands with Ned in quite a friendly way the wicked King turned to the giant. "Ha, ha!" he cried, "have I not had the pleasure of meeting you before, my fine friend?"

The giant said nothing, for what could he say?

"Have I not met you before?" repeated the King, with a fierce gesture. "Methinks you would look better as a pine tree than a hulking giant," and before the words were fairly out of the King's mouth a stately pine tree was standing in the courtyard, through which the wind of the early morning made a moaning noise much like the pitiful groan of the poor, late giant.

"And you, my little cockatoo," continued the wicked King, turning quickly to Ned, "would look better in a cage!"

And in another minute Ned found himself in a wicker cage, suspended from the lowest limb of the pine tree.

"And now," cried the wicked King, "where is your third guest?" The princess paused a moment. "Oh, the little bluebird!" she exclaimed, "where has it gone?"

"No, not the little bluebird, but he that was the bluebird."

At this the poor princess became very pale. She had hidden her brother the evening before when they had gone to bed in a closet in her room, hoping to have the opportunity of disguising him and sending him away with Ned and the giant the first thing in the morning. But, now, alas, her wicked stepfather undoubtedly suspected something. For else why should he ask for him?

She was in despair, for she knew not what to say. And where was Ned's little friend, the bluebird herself, all this time? Had she deserted her friends, the little princess asked herself?

"Answer my question!" cried the King, grasping hold of her wrist.

The princess screamed with terror and her brother, hearing her cry, rushed forth from the closet and down the stairs.

Whipping his sword from its scabbard, he made for the cruel tyrant.

Alas, that bravery and valor do not always win! It was useless for him to fight against so experienced a swordsman as the King, and in short time the prince was wounded and his sword thrown from his grasp.

"Little gamecock!" cried his conqueror, "you must needs grow larger spurs before you tackle an old rooster like me! And since you remind me of one, a rooster you shall be," and in five short seconds the little prince was changed into a young gamecock.

"Out into the courtyard!" cried the King; "a castle is no chicken house," and the little prince found himself unceremoniously thrown under the big pine tree.

"Have pity!" cried the little princess. "Is there no pity for a little orphan princess?"

"Enough," answered the King, with a stamp of his foot. "Go to your room, else you may find yourself also changed into a bird, or a tree, or a pretty butterfly."

So the unhappy little princess went up the stairs, crying bitterly, to her own chamber. Closing the door, she leaned out of the window and sobbed as if her heart would break.

For a moment she did not notice that the topmost branch of the pine tree was close to her casement. In fact, she would not have noticed it for some time probably, as her face was buried in her hands, had not the branch brushed against her fingers.

As she withdrew her hands from her face she heard the giant's voice, very much subdued, speaking to her.

"Ned says not to despair, for he feels sure that his little friend, the bluebird, will yet find a way to liberate us all."

THE MAGIC BALLOON

GREAT was the grief of the little bluebird as she skimmed over the waters of the moat, realizing how impossible it was for her to regain the lost ring.

She had not the heart for the moment to return to the castle to inform Ned of his loss; so she perched herself disconsolately on a bush which grew close to the margin of the moon-lit water, wondering what was best to do.

Suddenly the speckled trout rose to the surface, and, seeing how despondent was the pretty bluebird, inquired the cause of her grief.

"Ah, me!" she sighed in answer. "I have lost a magic gold ring, and I know not what to do, nor how to recover it."

At this the speckled trout flapped his silvery tail gleefully, and answered: "Worry no more, pretty bluebird, for I have it safely tucked away inside of me."

"If that be the case, Sir Trout," joyously chirped the happy bird, "swim at your greatest speed and deliver the ring to her majesty, the Waterfall Fairy, Queen of the Lake. Tell her that Ned, her little mortal friend, is in dire peril and that he needs her aid."

"That will I gladly do," answered the speckled trout, and without more delay he darted off down the moat toward the dam at the farther side, over which the water ran in a clear stream into the purling brook, which finally led to the lake, where lived Ned's friend, the Fairy Queen. Down the silvery cascade he glided and whirled away through the running water, frightening the minnows and miller's thumbs lying among the stones in the shallow places, and startling the crawfishes and little fresh water lobsters hidden under the hollow banks.

Faster and faster he swam, like a courier with important dispatches, down the clear stream running over its pebbly bed, with the luscious meadow sweet and the large blue geranium blooming all about its banks, and the wild rose on its bushes.

Nor did he pause until with a loud splash he dived over the waterfall safely into the lake and rose to the surface close to the palace of the Queen of the Lake.

A big black spider was busily at work mending the suspension bridge which spanned the water at this narrow point, for the heavy drops of dew had broken the slender strands in several places.

He stopped his work to look at the speckled trout, who at once addressed him.

"I am the bearer of a most important dispatch for her highness," he began.

"Well, and I am engaged in the most important duty of repairing her highness' bridge," replied the spider.

"So, I see," answered the trout, "but— —" At this very moment the Queen herself, hearing voices at so early an hour outside her window, peeped out. Catching sight of her the trout called out boldly:

"Listen to me, I beg of you, most gracious Queen. I have brought you the gold ring from Ned, who sorely needs thy aid!"

At this the Queen quickly withdrew her head, and in a short time emerged from the doorway of her castle.

Hastily running to the water's edge, she leaned over, grasping hold of a stalk to keep her from falling.

"Here is the ring," said the trout, holding it in his teeth and swimming as close to the bank as he was able.

The Queen reached out and took it safely from him.

"I will make you king of my fishes, noble Sir Trout," she cried, "for what you have this day accomplished. Remain here in my lake henceforth, and now, to the rescue!"

In an incredibly short time she was mounted on her swiftest robin and with her three ladies in waiting flew away toward the castle, where Ned and the beautiful princess, her brave brother and the giant were held prisoners by the magic of the wicked king.

Now, the little bluebird, as she saw her friend, the trout, swim away, suddenly thought of her former master, the King of the Gnomes, and decided to seek aid from him. So, whirling around in a circle to get her bearings, she darted off swiftly through the air toward the cave in the forest.

She made rapid progress until she reached the thick foliage of the woods, and here, in her eagerness, she nearly lost her way.

Indeed, in the uncertain light that struggled through the thick boughs, it was not easy to make out certain familiar landmarks which would guide her to her destination.

At length, just at dawn, she found herself at the foot of the hill wherein was the cave of the King of the Gnomes.

Worn out with her arduous journey, she fluttered down to the edge of the bubbling fountain and drank of its refreshing waters.

Then, picking up a pebble, she dropped it into the little gravelly basin, hopped painfully over to the great flat stone, and tapped upon it three times with her beak.

No one replied, but the rock opened in the middle, and there stood the King of the Gnomes himself.

On seeing the little bluebird, he stretched out a kindly hand for her to rest upon, and carried her into the inner room.

It was his breakfast hour, for gnomes are early risers. Seating himself at the table, he ordered that the little bird be served with breakfast at once, for well he knew that a hungry bird's first wish must be for food.

The King had scarce given this order before several nimble little men of the forest placed seeds and grains of wheat and a goblet of golden fruit juice before the bluebird.

Soon she was sufficiently revived to address the gnomes, and it took her but a few moments to tell him all.

"Come, let us hasten," he said, as she finished, and, slipping into his pocket his magic pipe and little pieces of soap, he left the cave and walked rapidly toward a small clearing.

Leaning over a little pool in the hollow of the grassy earth, he filled his pipe, rubbed the soap about the rim, and in a moment more blew a large soap bubble.

Taking the little bluebird in his hand, he opened a small door and entered the magic balloon. Up and up it went, until it was well above the tops of the trees.

Then it took a course toward the east, where the rising sun was gilding the sky with its golden fingers.

Faster and faster it sailed, overtaking in a short time the Fairy Queen and her three ladies-in-waiting, mounted on their friendly robins.

In the distance could be seen the turrets of the castle, gleaming in the morning sun like bayonets thrust up from the earth in monster guns.

"Now, little bluebird," said the Gnome, opening the little door and thrusting her out upon his hand, as the big Soap Bubble hovered above the castle, "fly down and tell Ned that deliverance is near at hand. So also inform the beautiful Princess, who, I see, is still sitting at her window, but asleep!"

Off flew the bluebird on her happy errand.

"Your Majesty," cried the Gnome, addressing the Fairy Queen, as she drew rein at the doorway of the soap bubble, "I would suggest that you touch with the Magic Ring only the cage wherein is confined our friend Ned, instructing him, while still in the form of a cockatoo, to fly up to the topmost branch of the pine tree. Also for the Princess' brother, while he is still a gamecock, to do likewise. After I have brought the bubble close to the window ledge, so that the beautiful Princess may step easily inside, I will cause it to rise to the treetop, from which advantageous position Ned and the Princess' brother can step within. But what to do with the Pine Tree Giant," said the Gnome, scratching his beard reflectively, "gets me!

However, one thing at a time, as my old grandfather used to say when I was a boy, 'one thing at a time!'"

As the bluebird whispered in the ear of the beautiful Princess, the Magic Soap Bubble approached the window ledge.

Rubbing her eyes, but making no outcry, although she was very much startled, she obeyed the bluebird's command to "step softly," and entered the Bubble. It then ascended till it was on a line with the topmost branch, where it swayed in the gentle morning breeze, like a barnyard weather cock, the game rooster on one side and the cockatoo on the other!

The Fairy Queen touched them with the ring as they hopped into the bubble, and they regained immediately their natural shape.

The Princess threw her arms around her dear brother and hugged Ned, so great was her delight.

Ned ran over to his little friend, the Gnome, and thanked him again and again for his aid, and was about to lean out of the doorway to also thank the Fairy Queen when the Gnome restrained him.

"Not so fast, Ned, my boy! All is not yet over."

"No, indeed," answered Ned, "we must rescue the giant."

"Aye, there's the rub," replied the Gnome. "How are we ever to get him in the bubble, either as a tree or as a giant?"

At this point the Fairy Queen joined in the conversation, kissing Ned at the same time as he attempted to thank her.

"Let me first change him into his natural form," she said. "Then he can walk across the courtyard and out upon the drawbridge. From there he can easily step off into the bubble, which your majesty can lower to the right height above the water of the moat."

"Good!" said the Gnome. "Go and do your part and I will attend to the bubble."

Just as the bubble cleared it the pine tree became once more the friendly giant, who immediately strode across the courtyard.

Quickly lowering the drawbridge he hastened out upon it.

The creaking of the chains, however, had aroused the wicked King, who looked out of his window to see what was the cause of the noise. In another moment he was rushing toward the gates at the head of the castle guard.

"Quick!" shouted the Gnome to the giant. "Get in!"

But, alas! The doorway was too small. In vain the giant wiggled and squirmed. In vain Ned and the princess' brother pulled his arms. His great shoulders could not be forced through the doorway. Finally, with a tremendous shove he managed to go half way in, but no further, for at this point his head was against the opposite side of the bubble.

On came the wicked King and his castle attendants, who, seeing the predicament of the giant, fitted arrows to their strong bows, preparing to shoot the hapless fellow.

"Blow the bubble larger!" shouted Ned. "Put the pipe in his mouth and tell him to blow like thunder."

The Gnome placed the pipestem between the lips of the giant and commanded him to blow for his life, and before an arrow left a bow the bubble widened sufficiently to enable the giant to crawl inside. Slamming the door shut the Gnome cried out exultingly: "We are safe!"

Away sailed the Magic Soap Bubble, with the Fairy Queen and her little robin perched securely on the top, and her three ladies in waiting standing close by on their own little feathered steeds.

Back to the beautiful Waterfall Lake, where the Fairy Queen bade Ned goodby; back to the friendly Gnome's cave in the woods, where he said farewell to Ned; back to Big Man's Land, where lived the Giant with his kind old mother; back to the castle where lived the beautiful Princess and her brother before the wicked King had kidnapped them, and back at last to Ned's own home, where it left him in the old easy chair by the window, from which he had started out to visit Gnomeland.

Well, well, little reader, here we are, you and I, at the end of the book. What shall we do, for we have grown to be such good friends while you have been reading this story of mine.

Listen, I will tell you another story, it's called "The Iceberg Express"—it is one of The Little Journeys to Happyland books. So come with me on the Iceberg Express.

Yours for a story,

DAVID CORY.